CATHLEEN

Companions of the Cattleman's Daughters

Danni Roan

Copyright © 2016 Danni Roan

All rights reserved

The characters and events portrayed in this book are fictitious. Any similarity to real persons, living or dead, is coincidental and not intended by the author.

No part of this book may be reproduced, or stored in a retrieval system, or transmitted in any form or by any means, electronic, mechanical, photocopying, recording, or otherwise, without express written permission of the publisher.

ISBN: 9798673834350

Cover design by: Erin Dameron-Hill
Library of Congress Control Number: 2018675309
Printed in the United States of America

To friendship that builds you up when you are down, makes family of strangers, and lends strength in weakness.

CONTENTS

Title Page
Copyright
Dedication
Prologue ... 1
Chapter 1 ... 3
Chapter 2 ... 11
Chapter 3 ... 20
Chapter 4 ... 26
Chapter 5 ... 33
Chapter 6 ... 42
Chapter 7 ... 50
Epilogue ... 60
Dear Reader, ... 65
About the Author ... 66

PROLOGUE

Cathleen Malone clutched the letter in her hand and gazed out across the dusty street of Casper Wyoming, trying to hold back the tears. Why had she listened to her father? Why had she given in to hope?

Silently she chewed her lower lip and desperately tried to think. What would she do now? How would she survive? She had nothing to go back to, nothing to look forward to. She was destitute and alone in a strange place. Her hands trembled, crumpling, and crackling the paper in her grasp.

Blinking back tears she looked down at the letter and marriage contract she held, the words had been so promising, such a lovely dream.

Casper Wyoming   May 16th, 1888

Dear Cathleen,

My name is Jared Romera and after reading your letter I believe that you are the perfect bride for me.

I'm a sheep farmer here in Wyoming and although I am not wealthy my place is doing well. I have a very nice, if small, house and a good barn with a few head of stock other than the sheep.

I am looking for a wife to cook and clean for me as well as share the long, lonely winter days and nights. I am tired of being alone with no one to talk to.

Looks don't mean much to me as long as you are hardworking and pleasant. I only know I don't want to spend another winter on my own with nothing but sheep to keep me company.

I hope that you will agree to be my wife,

Jared R.

He had said he didn't care about appearance, that he was looking for a companion, but apparently, he'd cared more than he realized, or perhaps no one could ever find her attractive. She should have known better but she'd promised her father she would try. She had promised him, as his dying wish, that she would find a new home with someone to love.

A lone tear escaped and spilled from the corner of her eye as the pain of rejection squeezed her heart.

CHAPTER 1

Benjamin Smith tucked his share of the cattle sale proceeds into his pocket and headed up the street toward the post office. It had been months since they'd been to town and the mail would be piling up. He had just turned the corner and stepped out into the street when looking up he spotted the most beautiful woman he'd ever seen standing alone on the train station platform.

His breath froze in his throat as he studied her. She was what his old friend Bridgette would have called buxom or full-figured but with curves in all the right places, a real armful. She had dark hair tucked up under a deep purple hat that matched a dress the color of ripe plums. Milky white skin was traced by soft lace trim that lifted the rounded neckline over her ample bosom in a modest but becoming fashion. Her heart-shaped face was offset by a straight nose, even brows and eyes so dark they seemed to pull him in, the way a loadstone pulls iron.

He watched chagrined as she worried her lower lip, turning her lush red lips a hue deeper than blood, the scarlet shades of a summer rose. His heart stuttered in his chest as a single tear slid down her soft pale cheek. His hand curled into fists as her obvious chagrin shot straight through his chest.

"Hey! Ya old fool! What ya doin' standing in the middle of the street!" A teamster yelled and cursed as his string of mules narrowly missed the older cowpuncher.

Benjamin jumped, sucking in a lung full of fresh air for the first time in what seemed like minutes. Setting his square jaw in determination Benjamin Smith strode to the platform, taking the stairs two at a time.

"Excuse me miss." He started gently, stepping as close to the lovely vision as propriety would allow. "I'm Benjamin Smith and I'd like to know if I could be of some assistance to you." He gazed at her, his deep blue eyes steady on her face as he drank in her pretty features.

He smiled as a light blush crept across the apples of her cheeks, and a breeze teased the soft strands of hair around her face. Benjamin clenched his fists tighter forcing his hands at his side so they wouldn't be tempted to brush the tendrils away from where they fluttered around her soft lips.

For a moment Cathleen just blinked back at the large gray-haired gentleman who had come to her aid. He was a tall man, over six feet tall with wide, beefy shoulders that tapered to narrow hips. He reminded her of a big bear standing on its back legs seeming to stoop ever so slightly in the middle, almost as if he were leaning forward in anticipation. His dark blue eyes were kind and he wasn't bad looking for a man in his fifties.

"Oh." She replied trying to decide what to do or say.

"You seem to be in some distress." The old cowpuncher offered again. "Can I help in any way?" His hand twitched toward her possessively, but he stopped it.

Cathleen's sardonic wit got the best of her and she snorted and then turned bright pink as she covered her mouth with a white-gloved hand.

The man smiled at her, eyes twinkling. She couldn't help but smile back.

"I'm afraid unless you have a spare husband in your back pocket, there isn't much you can do for me," her words were sharp and bitter. The tall man raised his brows.

Cathleen shook her head. "In for a penny in for a pound as my father used to say." She looked down at the letter in her hand. "I came here as a mail-order-bride, arriving only to find that my appearance was not satisfactory to my prospective groom, one Mr. Jasper Romera." Her eyes flashed for just a minute, with anger and hurt.

Her lips quirked in a bitter smirk as his exact words echoed through her mind. *"You never said you was fat. I can't be seen with a woman like you. You lied!"* His words had been cruel, angry, and life-shattering. He hadn't even given her a second glance as he stalked away leaving her alone in a strange place.

Shaking her head Cathleen watched in wonder as the older man's face transformed before her, emotions flickering from surprise to shock to anger in a matter of moments. She drew back as lightning flashed in his cobalt eyes.

"Are you tellin' me that a man brought you out here and now won't marry you?" he seemed genuinely astounded.

Cathleen nodded, then truly began to worry as the man before her, began to grin. He certainly was changeable in his moods.

"Then perhaps I can be of some assistance after all." He said, his eyes brightening as he stood to his full, impressive height.

Cathleen blinked at the aging cowhand, why would he help her? He didn't even know her, or what her true circumstances were.

"I'll marry you," he said with a smirk.

For a moment the dark-haired woman simply stared at him. Benji could tell she was going to argue and began to prepare his own words. She was everything he could ever want, he couldn't let her get away.

"You don't even know me?" She began.

"I'll get to know you," he countered.

"You'd never even laid eyes on me before now, why would you want to marry me?"

"You'd never seen your intended until just a little while ago, that didn't stop you."

For a moment anger flickered across his face. "Man like that should be horsewhipped for pure stupidity." He spoke as if to himself, before flicking a glanced across the street to where another white-haired man, of about his age, stood in front of the post office looking at them.

Cathleen couldn't help it, she smiled. "But..." she began again.

"But what?" He asked not unkindly. "Do you have any better prospects? Or perhaps a family to return to back home?" He studied her face as it betrayed the truth in every line before her luminous eyes fell.

"No," she whispered.

"Then why not me? I know I'm no dashing young man, but I have a good home and friends who are like family to me." His eyes flicked back across the street but the other man was gone. "I can provide for you and keep you safe. What more could anyone ask for?" He finished logically.

Yes, what more? Cathleen thought, perhaps a chance at love.

"But what could I bring to you?" her words were so soft a gentle breeze would have snatched them away.

Benjamin Smith looked her up and down, feeling somehow younger than his fifty-six years. He swallowed hard to keep the words in his head at bay. Instead, he looked her in the eye and said "Companionship." He had to bite the inside of his cheek to keep from smiling at her sudden blush.

"These your things?" He asked suddenly, changing the subject as he glanced at her bags. Cathleen blinked at him as he indicated the two tattered carpet bags by her feet.

"Yes." She answered wondering what he would do next.

"Got anything else?" His gaze was direct, his bright eyes serious.

"No." What could he be thinking? She blinked as he bent down and lifted both heavy cases easily then stuck out his elbow to her.

"Good, now how's about we go get a nice cup of coffee and a piece of pie and we'll see if we can come to some agreement." He looked at her intently over his left shoulder expecting her to obey.

Silently lifting a prayer heavenward, she slipped her gloved hand into the crook of his arm and walked down the stairs.

The little restaurant he took her to was a small one-room affair with a kitchen outback. Small square tables set for four were strategically situated around the room just far enough away to allow a private conversation as well as space for the serving girls to move about freely.

Benjamin escorted his female companion to a table, pulled out a chair for her then sat. He smiled at her hoping she'd agree to his proposal once she had a little time to get to know him. He'd be heading back to the Broken J the next day and didn't have much time so he whispered a little prayer that she'd be with him when he left Casper.

"This place is just about brand new." He offered, "Casper hasn't been a town proper for long but with the railroad arriving last year it's buildin' up fast." He smiled trying to put her at ease. "Used to just be a place to cross the South Platte River and a fort, but now look at it."

A serving girl arrived and he ordered coffee along with a slice of cherry pie for himself then looked at the woman across the table, who only ordered coffee which surprised him. He would have thought she'd be hungry after a long trip on the train. Then again he didn't know how far she'd come.

"I thought we could have a little talk and get to know each other a bit then you can decide if I'm an acceptable alternative to, well whatever alternative you might have." He looked at her again expectantly.

Cathleen squirmed in her seat. She was tired, dirty, hungry, and as much as she hated to admit it heart sick. What could she do? She felt completely useless.

"Just tell me a little about yourself." The man called Benjamin suggested a gentle smile on his rugged face.

Her eyes grew wide as she realized she'd never even told this man her name.

"I'm Cathleen Malone," she said keeping her voice steady with an effort. "I come from Ohio where my father was a dairy farmer." She brushed at her lovely dress but said no more.

"I'm Benjamin Smith like I said earlier but most folks call me Benji." The server returned delivering their coffee and a single piece of pie. "I'm the current foreman of the Broken J ranch about a four-day ride from Casper." A strange look passed over his face when he mentioned his job making Cathleen wonder if he didn't like what he did.

"If you don't mind my asking why did you choose to be a mail-order-bride?" His eyes were still soft as he studied her face taking the bite from his words, but they still felt so much like an accusation to her.

"Before my father died he wanted me to find someone who would look after me." Her voice was soft, embarrassed by all of the implications of becoming a mail-order-bride suggested. "I didn't have anywhere else to go." She let her words end there.

Benji reached out a hand and placed it over hers. "I'm sorry for your loss." She was surprised to hear the sincerity in his voice. His hand was warm and comforting.

"So you don't have anywhere else to go?" he asked still looking at her as if he cared.

"No, I'm afraid I don't."

The smile that brightened his face was contagious and she couldn't help but smile back at him shyly. He was a good person, somehow she was sure of that fact, even if she didn't know why she believed it.

"Well, then there's no reason you can't marry me." His eyes were hopeful. "I've got a home and friends and everything you might need. It ain't fancy but it's home."

She knew he was just being kind and felt she should decline. He hadn't ordered a bride.

"I'm sure you don't want to marry me," she replied, surprised when his eyes widened.

"Why not? You seem like a good God-fearing woman, you're pretty, and I assume you can cook."

A splash of bright color crossed her cheeks. "Now I know you're just being kind."

"Why would I do that?" Benji answered. "I'm a single man and you're a single woman so why not just get hitched?" He looked at her again. "We can go over to the preacher and get married. Easy as that."

Benjamin watched hopefully as the dark-haired woman studied her coffee cup. There were streaks of gray in her hair, especially near her face and he found it becoming. She wasn't a blossoming youth but a mature woman. Perhaps not as old as he was but old enough to be interesting company for an aged bachelor.

"If you think you can stand to have me. I don't have any other options," Cathleen finally said not raising her eyes.

Benji smiled despite the sadness he felt at her resigned tone. She was such a beautiful woman, perhaps no longer young, if he guessed right she was probably in her early forties, but he wished she would believe him when he said he wanted her.

CHAPTER 2

The next day Benjamin helped Cathleen up into the high seat of a big freight wagon then scrabbled around to the other side to take the reins of the four-horse team.

"Ready?" he asked looking at her with his dark blue eyes. She nodded, smoothing the skirt of her fancy purple dress.

Cathleen looked out across the wild frontier town taking in the buildings with wonder. She'd never seen anything like it, low buildings ran the length of the dusty street, the largest one the mercantile they'd just left.

The man beside her shook the reins and the wagon lurched as they started out of town. There were several buildings and more going up even as they drove through the town. Many of the buildings were just tents and people milled about the town either getting off the train or moving cattle toward the stockyards.

The horses clopped along the dusty street headed toward the crossing of the Platte River. As they came out onto open prairie she could see the line of wagons and carts waiting to cross. It was the first crossing on the river and the town, originally just a camp for the

bridge was growing. The rail station bringing more travelers or settlers by the day.

Cathleen was surprised when her new husband turned away from the bridge and headed toward a small group of people further out along the road. A large green wagon was the first item she could make out, but as they approached she noticed several men sitting on horses milling around.

Benjamin clicked to the horses and they stepped into a trot making the seat bounce. She laid a hand over her décolletage modestly but smiled despite herself.

"Benji!" several people called as they approached. She gasped when a young woman dressed like a cowhand trotted up along the wagon, a curious look on her pretty face and a long coppery braid dangling down her back.

"Mornin' Meg," Benjamin called, but kept driving. As he reached the gathering, a tall white-haired man sitting on a big buckskin horse turned toward them. Cathleen blinked recognizing him as the man from the post office the day before. He pulled his horse up short, his eyes widened at the sight of her on the wagon seat.

"Joshua." Benjamin's voice boomed out, humor oozing through his words. "I'd like you to meet Cathleen, my wife." He smiled broadly, a wicked twinkle in his eyes.

The only sound in the whole camp was the jingle of harness and the stamp and snort of horses.

Cathleen blushed as all eyes turned toward her. The man on the buckskin horse was the first to recover from the shock pushing his horse toward the wagon and lifting his hat from his head.

"Pleased to meet you, Mrs. Smith," he said a hearty grin spreading across his face making his startling ice-blue eyes sparkle. "I'm Joshua James of the Broken J ranch and this is my family, welcome aboard."

Cathleen took a deep breath. There were so many people. Three more girls rode up to the wagon gaping at her, two, with deep chestnut hair and dark brown eyes, were twins. While another slightly taller girl had a sweet face and unruly dark curls, streaked with blonde, that even this early in the morning were straining to be free of their braid.

"I'm Fiona" the curly-haired girl called up to Cathleen with a smile. "This is Lexi." She pointed to one of the twins whose dark brown eyes and dark hair gleamed in the early rays of the sun. "and Issy." She indicated the other twin. "We're Josh's daughters." Her voice was kind and helped to put Cathleen at ease. The other girls nodded toward her in polite greeting.

"I'm Muiread," the girl with the copper locks called as she pulled her chestnut horse in line with her sisters. "Call me Meg though." She smiled then looked toward her father.

"I reckon you can get to meet everyone else as we go. I'm sure Benji will fill you in on who's who either way." Joshua James smiled up at her then turning his horse toward the west, lifting a hand. "Let's head home," he called pushing his horse into an easy walk.

Cathleen watched as an old green wagon, it's high rounded covered top lurching and swaying over the rutted road, set the pace. Her husband, she glanced at him still unsure how she felt about that, snapped the reins on his team, and fell in line behind the other conveyance. Around them, men, women, and horses fell in line as they started down the trail.

For a long time, Cathleen gazed at the road ahead. The land was flat and at this time of year dry, with grasses beginning to turn from lush green to light gold. In the far distance, she could see the mountains. Before leaving her home in Youngstown she'd scoured the old papers in the library looking for information on Wyoming. At least she was used to wide-open spaces, cold winters, and cows.

Benji glanced at his new wife, his heart skipping up a beat at her pretty face and soft shapely body. He wanted to reach out and take her hand to reassure her that she'd made the right choice by marrying him. He knew he was older than she was but already he felt like a new man just having her sitting on the high bench next to him, looking so lovely. He wondered what she was thinking as she looked out over the prairie.

Cathleen wondered what the man next to her was thinking. He was kind to take her in as he had. She hoped she wouldn't be an embarrassment to him and that she'd be able to help him at the home he'd told her about the night before. Her heart dropped as she remembered her wedding night. It was not what every girl dreamed.

***

Casper Wyoming,   August 12, 1888

Cathleen took the arm of the bear of a man who'd convinced her that her only option was to marry him. She shouldn't have needed convincing she truly had no alternatives, but he'd taken the time to talk to her just the same. Her insides quivered as she realized she was putting her life into the hands of this big, soft-eyed stranger.

"Here's the preacher." Benjamin Smith said softly as they stopped in front of a stiff-looking white tent. "He ain't been here long so no real digs yet. I hope you don't mind."

"No, no," she said a bit surprised that the town didn't have a real church.

"Are you ready?" He asked, patting her hand where it rested in the crook of his arm.

Cathleen took a deep breath and forced a smile. She'd known she'd be marrying right away when she arrived in Casper, she just hadn't known it would be out of pity. Nodding she stepped through the tent flap that the graying man held open for her.

The ceremony was short and direct. Nothing like the weddings of her few friends back East. The preacher asked them questions and they answered in the affirmative. He then, rather off-handedly said the words every bride is waiting for on her wedding day. "You may kiss the bride." The parson spoke while taking the marriage contract out of her hand and signing it with a flourish.

Benjamin Smith turned to the lovely vision, who had just become his wife and smiling dipped his head to hers brushing her lips with a chaste kiss. He wanted much more but didn't want to frighten her.

The preacher handed back the contract and they both realized that one name was wrong on it. Benjamin quickly scrawled his name over the name of Jared Romera with a smile then took Cathleen's hand. He couldn't believe his luck.

Not wanting to subject the weary woman to the whole crew of the Broken J on her first day he quickly decided to take her to a small house he knew of that would give you a hot meal and rent you a room for a night. Then he'd take some time and get to know his lovely bride.

Benjamin escorted Cathleen to a small home near the outskirts of town. It was no more than a four-room cabin with a shake roof and dusty yard, but who was she to complain. She'd spent the last six days on the hard bench of a train.

"We'll stay here tonight, and then meet up with everyone in the morning. I'm sure you're tired after your long journey," Benjamin spoke, ushering her into the humble building with a warm hand on her back.

The meal, served at a communal table, was simple but delicious. A hearty stew with thick slices of bread to go with it. Cathleen was hungry but embarrassed to show it. She delicately picked at her food not wanting to let her new husband think she was unrestrained or gluttonous.

"Aren't you hungry?" That very man, seated next to her, asked. "Or maybe you don't like it. I can get us something else." He seemed truly concerned.

"No it's very good," she replied hastily, "I think I'm just tired."

His soft smile made her breath a little easier. "You'll need your strength for the drive ahead so I'd suggest you eat up, we won't be eating this good on the trail, especially with Old Billy doing the cooking."

Cathleen smiled back at him as he encouraged her to enjoy her meal then tucked into the food. He didn't seem to mind that she didn't eat like a bird, she truly hoped it was all right because, in reality, she was famished.

After their meal he led her to one of the four bedrooms where a large galvanized tub had been set on the floor next to the big double bed, soft steam creating a haze above it.

"Oh, there you are," their hostess Mrs. Wilkes said. "I got that bath ready just like you asked Mr. Smith." She smiled at Benji who reached into his pocket and handed her a coin.

"Thank you, Mrs. Wilkes," he said kindly, turning to Cathleen as the widow Wilkes stepped out of the room. "I thought you might like a hot bath before we hit the trail tomorrow. I hope that's all right." His dark blue eyes looked hopeful, like a boy eager to see if his gift was good enough.

"Oh, yes, thank you so much!" Cathleen replied excitedly. "I feel like half my being is made up of soot and smoke." Her smile was bright and for just a moment Benji could see the twinkle that he knew belonged in her eyes.

"I'll be stepping outside so you can be private." His voice was husky. "Tomorrow we'll stop at the mercantile to collect the supply order and pick you up a few things before we hit the trail," he finished stepping backward through the door and closing it with a snap.

Cathleen Malone, no Cathleen Smith let out a deep breath and allowed her whole body to slump. She was exhausted, filthy, and heart-sore, not to mention a nervous wreck over this whole ordeal. How had everything gotten so topsy-turvy? Pushing the thought away, she unhooked the clasps at her back letting the deep plumb gown, she'd worn for days, drop to the floor. She then hurried to unlace her corset, dropping it with a contented sigh. Next, came her petticoats, bloomers, camisole, stockings, and shoes.

The hot water felt like heaven on earth, not wasting any time she picked up a cloth and a bar of soap that smelled of honey and lemon, scrubbing herself thoroughly.

The sweet smell of the soap and the warm water was soothing, and she wondered where such a lovely item had come from. She felt cramped in the tub, but being clean felt wonderful. After a good scrub, she stood, dried her body then bending over the tub pushed her mass of straight dark hair into the water, lathering it with the same soap then rinsing it with the pitcher that stood by the tub, wringing her hair out then wrapping it in another bit of toweling felt glorious.

Once she was fully clean she rummaged in her bag for her best nightgown. It was getting thread bear along the cuffs and she'd have to make a new one soon but she pulled the soft white fabric over her head and taking a silver-backed brush from her bag began brushing out her hair so it would dry.

A soft knock on the door made Cathleen jump. "Yes," she answered just loud enough to be heard.

The door swung open and Benjamin Smith stepped in. His eyes raked up and down her body a surprised look on his face as he swallowed then spoke.

"I'll...I'll just take the water out," he stammered his voice gruff as he blinked at Cathleen's soft blush.

Moving across the room Benji lifted the tub and carefully carried it out the door. Cathleen was surprised at the strength he still had at his age.

A few minutes later he returned, standing nervously in the middle of the room as she tied her hair into a braid that fell well below her hips.

"You must be tired," he finally offered. "You go ahead and take the bed and I'll just kip on the floor." He turned his words into actions as he pulled a pillow from the bed and a quilt from a rack on the wall.

Cathleen's heart stuttered. She'd been right he was just a kind man who was taking her in. He didn't find her attractive or truly want her as a wife. She felt her lower lip tremble as she blew out the lamp and climbed into the bed alone. This was not the wedding night she had hoped for. She couldn't blame him if he didn't want her, she understood, no one else had ever wanted her either, not in all of her forty-two years. She'd never been courted and thought she didn't care, but somehow the fact stung.

A silent tear ran down her cheek as she pulled the blankets tight.

Benji eased himself onto the hard floor with a shiver. He could tell that Cathleen was crying. She must have had her heart set on that Jared fellow. He growled in his chest wishing he could find the man and give him a good beating for hurting his Cathleen. He started, wondering when he'd begun to think of her as his. He felt protective of his new bride even as he wished with every inch of his being that he was in that bed with her now.

Walking in earlier and seeing Cathleen sitting on the quilt, her long hair falling across her shoulders over the thin muslin of her nightgown had nearly stopped his heart. His whole body heated to boiling point in that instance as his eyes lingered on her full bosom straining the light fabric. It had taken all of his will power not to lay her back on the bed and kiss her senseless. He groaned just thinking about it. He wanted to feel her in his arms, and get lost in the ripe fullness of her body.

Maybe that skinner was right, he thought as he tried to find a comfortable position on the hard wooden planks. *Maybe I am just an old fool.*

CHAPTER 3

An especially bad rut in the road jostled Cathleen causing her to squeal and grab the seat, startling her back to the present. A strong hand reached out steadying her and she looked up into the smiling eyes of Benjamin Smith. She smiled back, thinking how silly she would have looked tumbling top over tea kettle into the dirt.

"You all right?" the man asked, his arm still around her shoulders. She scooted closer to him on the seat so he didn't have to stretch so far.

"Yes," she smiled again, "I can't help but think that my tumbling off this wagon would have left a lasting first impression on everyone from the Broken J." her eyes sparkled.

Benji smiled. "You've been very quiet is there anything you need? I'm afraid it will be a while before we can stop."

"I was just thinking." Cathleen replied, "It's been a strange few days." Growing quiet, her mind went back to her first night as Mrs. Smith.

***

Cathleen awakened in the little room to find that Benjamin had already gone. Her heart raced surely he hadn't married her just to decide he couldn't stand to be with her now. What would she do? How would she survive? The rejection of the day before threatened to panic her.

Pulling herself together she rose and dressed. The door opened again just as she was lacing up her shoes. She sighed in relief when the burly man stepped through the door.

"Good, you're up." He'd smiled at her. "Mrs. Wilkes has breakfast ready and then we'll head to the store."

"Thank you," her voice was shaky even to her own ears as she stepped toward the washbasin. "I'll be ready in a minute."

Benjamin moved closer to her looking down at her. Taking her face in his hands, his face showed concern. "I'm not going anywhere you know that don't you?" he said softly. "You don't have to worry, I'll take care of you."

She smiled at him weakly. "I'll be right out."

As her new groom exited the room she stood before the small washbasin, splashed water on her face, and looked at herself in the mirror.

"Enough of this," she demanded of the reflection. "You will make the best of this situation. You knew you were not marrying for love so one situation is just as good as the other."

She glared at the woman before her. She was forty-two and had never been courted she didn't need any romantic nonsense now. She would have a home, people who would become friends and a kind man to see that she was safe and provided for even if he wasn't attracted to her.

"It will do," she stated then straitening her hair she picked up her bag and stepped out the door into her new life.

***

"Cathleen?" Her husband's voice drew her voice back to the present. "I know this must be a difficult trip for a lady like yourself. You'll be more comfortable when we get to the ranch."

Cathleen gaped. Why would he think she was a lady? She looked down at her clothes, at the fine dress that she had been given just before she left Ohio. Bernice, the matchmaker had insisted she have one good gown. She'd given her the hat and the parasol as well. Cathleen smiled remembering, before fear gripped her heart, what if Benjamin thought she'd deceived him, what if he was disappointed when she explained? Her heart thumped in her chest, but she placed a hand on his arm.

"I'm not a lady," she said looking at him closely. "I'm just a girl from a farm. Please don't be upset?"

"Why would I be upset?" the man asked seriously.

"You thought I was a lady because of this fancy dress and I'm not. I didn't mean to deceive you."

"Just because I assumed something doesn't mean you deceived me. Even if you are a girl from a farm you're a lady in my eyes."

Cathleen was surprised. He didn't seem to mind at all.

"Why don't you tell me a little about yourself while we travel? We've got four days on the road to get to know each other better."

Cathleen didn't know what to say, what was there to tell? She was a simple girl with little experience of the world. She'd grown up on the dairy farm her father worked until his death just three months ago. Her mother had gone on to glory years earlier.

"Tell me how you came to be here in Wyoming?" the drover next to her prompted, leaning his elbows on his knees while holding loosely to the reins in his hands.

"My father worked on a large dairy farm in Youngstown Ohio for his whole life," she began. "We didn't own it but we did have a little house to stay in." She smiled thinking about it.

"I kept house for my father after my mother passed away when I was twelve. It was a simple life but we were content." She glanced at the man called Benjamin beside her. "I never married," her words were soft almost embarrassed.

Benji wondered about her last statement. It seemed impossible a lovely woman like this with such a fetching smile could become a spinster. He frowned, thinking on it, but kept quiet.

"When Papa got ill he worried about what I would do. I knew I could have stayed on as a milkmaid at the farm but he wanted more for me. He told me I should marry and have a home of my own." She smiled her eyes taking on a far off look.

"So you like cows?" Benjamin's voice interrupted her thoughts.

"Oh yes." She replied. "They're daft, and you get a mean one now and then but overall I like them. I had better since I've spent the last forty-two years around them." She blushed scarlet suddenly realizing she'd revealed her age.

Cathleen cut her eyes toward the man she called husband, hoping he hadn't noticed. He smiled brightly at her but without any sign of doubt in his eyes.

"Cows are a little different on the ranch than what you'd be used to," he offered. "We do have two good milk cows but the rest are beef animals and are mostly out on the range." Benji looked at her checking that she understood. "We just delivered a large herd to Casper to ship off to market so the round-up and drive for the season is over."

They rode along in companionable silence for a while before Benji spoke again.

"So how did you come to be a mail-order-bride?" he asked.

"A few of the women from town decided to become mail-order-brides." Cathleen began. "When Papa was ill he asked me to write to the matchmaker so I did."

Benjamin Smith noticed how her shoulders slumped and he

knew she was thinking about that dunder-head that had left her at the station. Gently he wrapped an arm around her and squeezed. She felt so warm, so soft. He sighed wishing he could wrap both arms around her and kiss her.

Cathleen scooted closer to the man next to her. Her hip brushed his, she longed for human contact even just that little bit. It had been so long since anyone had held her tight. She was glad she had married a kind man, even if he didn't desire her.

A wheel hit a rock in the road and one of the lines jerked from Benji's hand slapping the near horse on the rump and causing him to jump. In an instant, all four animals lurched into a run spooked by the sudden movement.

Benji, grabbed for the reins as they slithered toward the foot rail at the front of the big wagon, catching them just in time but his sudden movement made the horses lurch forward faster. Bracing his feet against the foot rail, Benjamin hauled on the reins, calling to the horses, in a calm voice, even as he struggled to gain control.

"Whoa, whoa," He cried keeping his voice gentle while he jiggered the reins bringing the horses back to a slow walk. "You all right?" He asked looking intently at the woman next to him who had a death grip on the bench seat.

Slowly Cathleen let go of the seat, her eyes wide as she gazed at him and a smile spread across her face. "Nothing like a brisk run in the mornin' to get you going," she said and chuckled.

Benji laughed. "I'm sorry if I scared you." He was delighted that she hadn't fallen into hysterics.

"No harm done, so it's as good as if it didn't happen." She said, her eyes still bright from the excitement.

"Benji?" Joshua's voice called up to them as he reined his big buckskin in by the wagon.

"I lost a rein," Benji replied his face heating. "Must have gotten distracted." He winked at Cathleen, who smiled.

To Cathleen's surprise, the other man laughed his arctic eyes twinkling in merriment. "Can't imagine why?" he snorted then turned his horse back to the trail.

Benji, face flushed, turned back to his bride. "I'll be more careful," he offered, squeezing her hand. His face darkened further as the rest of the group rode by eyeing them with quick grins.

Snapping the reins, he clicked to the team and started off again.

CHAPTER 4

The rest of the ride to the Broken J ranch was uneventful. Little by little Cathleen learned who each person was as they took turns riding along with the big wagon. She was amazed at the girls who rode like men and found the youngest one, Mae, a delightful distraction from the constant plodding of the wagon.

The girl, full of energy and excitement at her first drive to town, would charge up along the wagon, her black hair flying in the wind created by her pinto pony, and simply call up to Cathleen on a whim. Her excited voice would point out things of interest or just chatter about how much there had been to see in Casper. Each encounter left Cathleen more interested in her new home.

Benjamin, always attentive, did his best to introduce her to everyone as well. Walters, she learned, was the thin bald wrangler and Stevens or Steve for short was the average-sized cowpoke who was slow to speak but a top hand.

"We all came out here with Joshua and his first wife Bridgette," Benjamin explained to her as they bedded down that night in the wagon. She noticed how he was careful to keep a distance between them even in the close confines of the heavily loaded wagon which brought back some of the sadness of the night before. She understood she hadn't married for love but some affection would have been nice. Pushing the thoughts away she concentrated on what her husband was saying.

"Josh's first wife got ill carrying Fiona and so he just up and left the wagon train we were on headin' to Oregon. He took a look at the Big Basin and the far away Wind River Mountains and just said he was stoppin'. Me, Steve an' Walt plus a couple more including Billy, just decided to stay as well. We're all that's left from that original bunch now."

"Why would you stay with them, the James' I mean? Weren't you going to Oregon?" Cathleen asked, surprised at the loyalty the men had shown.

"Well, Josh al'ays seemed to have big ideas." Benjamin scratched his head thinking about the subject. "He talked about setting up a farm and maybe getting people to stake claims close enough that they could kinda' look out for each other. That way with the land grants it would be one big place with folks workin' to help out instead of one small bit with one fella trying to make a go." He paused thinking a minute. "Josh's an easy goin' type but he's a thinker. It didn't hurt that he got us out of a few scrapes along the way, so when he decided this was good land to put down roots we figured it was as good as any other." He smiled ruefully then. "Besides we was pretty fond of them girls of his. Pretty much tired of the trail."

Cathleen took some time to think about everything she'd learned about the ranch and all of the people she'd met so far. "It's all still rather confusing," she admitted honestly. "I'll have to see if it gets better when I meet everyone at the ranch." Inside her stomach turned with worry. What if she didn't fit in?

It was almost three days later when they turned the big open rig toward an arched gateway that led to a compound spread out inside a fenced yard. The first thing to come into view was the windmill near the big barn, then the house, a large gray, two-story home with a wrap-around porch and tin roof. It was bigger than she had expected.

The closer they got the more excited all of the girls became pointing things out to the newcomer as they approached. That morning each girl had decided to change into their dresses and ride in the wagon on top of the supplies for the last stretch home, and their excited chatter was contagious.

"That's the sod shack to the left," Mae announced from the top of a barrel of flour in the back of the wagon.

"You can't see them from here but there's a chicken coop and the blacksmith's shop around the corner of the barn and the bunkhouse is the long building that backs the fence on the far side of the house." She continued, pointing in the direction of each building she named. "There's even a bathhouse" she whispered with a grin.

"I can't wait to see Nona's face when she meets you." The teenaged girl giggled and her sisters smiled back.

As they pulled into the ranch yard Cathleen's anxiety levels grew. There were already so many people just on the drive and she knew from what Benjamin had said there were at least five more to meet. She twisted a handkerchief nervously in her hands as a pretty golden-haired young woman in her early twenties and a tall lanky cowboy burst onto the front porch.

"Pa!" the girl called before realizing that Benji sat on the seat of the wagon, her eyes traveling up the side of the conveyance to gawk at Cathleen who blushed.

Beside her, Benji was grinning devilishly, "Hello, darling." His deep voice was full of humor. "I wanted to be the first to introduce you to my lovely wife Cathleen." His eyes twinkled at the look on her face.

Cathleen could see the shock on the young woman's face and as much as she could appreciate the humor in Benjamin dropping that bombshell she felt conspicuous, and out of place. What would this tight-knit group think of one of their own bringing home a stranger?

The other girls poured from the wagon, squealing with delight as they rushed to their sister and swept her into the house, chattering and gossiping all at once.

Cathleen watched the girls disappear through the door of the big house as the cowboy stepped down from the steps, tipped his hat, and began to collect the horses from the tired riders.

Benjamin climbed down from the big wagon then walking around helped Cathleen down from the seat. Holding her hand, he started toward the house, but before they'd even reached the stairs a plump woman with graying hair and dark eyes rushed out onto the porch arms raised above her head shouting at the top of her voice.

"Algori! Algori!" Her accented voice called as she raced down the stairs, throwing her arms around Cathleen nearly knocking the wind out of her lungs. "Congratulations!" she called again.

Cathleen cut her eyes to her husband of four days a frightened expression on her face as she struggled to stay calm, but Benjamin smiled brightly and pulled the other woman off of her.

"Bianca, don't strangle her. This is my new wife Cathleen." Benji chuckled, squeezing Cathleen's hand. "I'm sure you'll both get well acquainted soon enough but for now I need to get the soddy in shape so we can move in tonight".

"What?" the woman called Bianca screeched. "No, no, no! You will take the spare room upstairs." She turned and walked toward the house Benji right on her heels.

"Bianca, we are staying in the sod shack. We've already decided."

"No." the portly woman wheeled by the stairwell just visible inside the house, placing her hands on her hips and preparing for a full-on attack.

"I said we're goin' to the soddy and we're goin'!" Benji shouted. "Now you can either help me or not, it's up to you."

Cathleen watched horrified by the scene playing out before her. She had only been on the ranch for minutes and already there was turmoil. She could feel the bright color rising her, neck and on to her face mingling with the heat of a summer day.

Peeking over her shoulder from where she still stood on the front porch she saw another man come down the long corridor and lay a weathered hand on the older woman's shoulder. He was a smaller man than Benjamin but executed a sense of quiet calm. His dark eyes, kind but sharp.

"Leave it, Bia," he said gently. "Benji's a grown man and has a right to his own decisions." Bianca Leoné's, known as Nona to the James' girls, mouth hung open for just a moment before she closed it with a snap, and as quick as her temper had come up it was gone.

"Well Benjamin if you insist, I was just thinking of your new bride is all." Her look was indignant but there was no meanness in her voice. "She looks such a lady and to have to stay in the soddy…" Her voice trailed off as she saw the woman of whom she spoke standing slump-shouldered with embarrassment on the front porch.

Nona's face softened turning a distinctive shade of pink. Then with one nod of her head, she turned and shouted up the stairs for the girls, an all too familiar tone in her voice, and with that tenor of voice, the girls scrambled down the stairs to await their marching orders.

Benjamin Smith turned to see his new wife sagging with mortification over the confrontation that had just occurred. He knew it would be hard for her to settle in at the Broken J with its boisterous family atmosphere but he didn't think it would start like this. He shot a glare at Bianca Leoné', Joshua's mother-in-law, then stepped out onto the porch to wrap an arm around the beautiful woman he called his own.

Talking to her softly he staved off the tears that threatened to fall. "I'm afraid it's always like this here."

"I didn't mean to be so much trouble," Cathleen whispered.

"You're no trouble." The plump woman joined them with a soft smile on her face. "We can be a little outspoken around here, that's all." Gently she put an arm around Cathleen. "You come along and have a cup of tea while we get the sod shack cleared out for you." She smiled again but cut a black look at Benji as if all of this was his fault.

"You go on with Bia," he said leaning forward and kissing Cathleen on the forehead. "I'll see that our new home gets settled, then help put up the supplies."

Cathleen was hustled down a corridor along the stairwell and into a large kitchen that ran nearly the length of the house, then through a doorway and ushered to a small drop leaf table sitting near the wall under a window. Outside she could see another long back porch that was mostly taken up by two large tables.

"You just sit down," the other woman spoke "and I'll get us some tea," she added as she bustled over to a large stove on the other side of the kitchen, its green enamel bright, before moving the kettle to the center of the stove.

"You must be completely worn out," the woman called Bianca spoke as she pulled down cups and saucers, milk and sugar, and a heavy black teapot. "Don't you worry about a thing either," the woman continued as she moved efficiently around the kitchen eventually laying a plate of cookies on the table before filling the teapot. "The girls and I will come along and make that place shipshape for you tomorrow. I don't know why Benji insists on you stayin' out dere." She shook her head and tsked.

Cathleen noticed the grimace the woman made at mention of

the shod shack. "I'm sure it will be fine. I'm just happy we're no longer on the trail. I feel like I've been on the move forever." She smiled trying to show that she was pleased to be here and with her living arrangements, she didn't want to be a bother.

The short rounded woman finally came to rest at the table with a sigh and began pouring tea. "If Benji had let us know you were coming it would have been easier," she said but smiled brightly and impulsively reached out to take Cathleen's hand. "Welcome to the Broken J dear." She added sipping her tea.

CHAPTER 5

After tea and cookies, where Bianca chattered away at her, Cathleen was escorted to what everyone called the soddy and finally stepped into the little earthen building that would be her new home. She'd never been in a sod building before and couldn't help but wonder what it could be like. The first thing she noticed was the overwhelming smell of apples. The apples harvested from the few trees that grew behind the bunkhouse had been, until just hours ago, stored in the small dry hut. It was blessedly cool no matter what it smelled of, and she smiled.

She'd been surprised when a wizened old Chinese man had come to escort her to the shack with Mae at his side. "This is my Ye-ye," The girl spoke up. "My great-grandfather." She smiled and the old man's dark eyes twinkled back at her with affection.

"I take you to your new house." He'd offered, extending a hand toward the back door. "It all ready for you now." He added with a wink.

Cathleen couldn't help but grin at the mischievous gleam in his old eyes. Even at his age, he seemed to exude energy.

A steady stream of people carrying furniture, bedding, and a plethora of other household items suddenly stopped their coming and going, leaving her mercifully alone in the tiny space, to take in her surroundings.

The little house was approximately twenty feet by twenty feet and almost square. To her right pushed up against the rolled earthen walls sat a minuscule round potbellied stove next to a small shelf with pegs for mugs, and a short bench with a wash bucket on it.

Directly in front of the stove was a small square table just big enough for two people with two mismatched chairs. The other side of the building held a large wooden bed now covered in a bright quilt of red and yellow patches.

A small window was suspended over the bed on the far wall that faced the ranch yard and along the wall near the door stood a bench with a row of pegs on the wall to hang clothing items.

Cathleen smiled. It was small and snug and cozy. She glanced up at the ceiling surprised to see wooden beams supporting the earthen roof. "This will do just fine." She said to herself looking around more closely, before stamping her foot on the hard-packed dirt floor, surprised at its firmness. Overall, it was lovely and surprisingly pretty with its plastered walls.

She turned as the door opened again and several of the James girls came in carrying more items from the main house. "Oh," the oldest Katie exclaimed. "We thought you were still with Nona."

At Cathleen's confused look, the golden-haired girl smiled. "We all call Bianca Nona. It means grandmother in Italian." She smiled again. "We brought a coffee pot, skillet, and a bucket to scrub things up. I'm Katie by the way," she added.

"Thank you girls, you've all been so lovely." Cathleen said shyly "but you've done enough. This will be my home and I'll take it from here." She felt both determined and embarrassed at the same time. Everyone had done more than enough for her it was time she got started on doing for herself.

"Oh we couldn't let you do that," Katie began.

"I'm afraid you don't have a choice," Cathleen countered. "I've done next to nothing so far and I need to be active. You leave everything with me and I'll take it from here." Her voice left room for no argument. She was surprised that Katie didn't say anything though as she looked up and down at the fine dress the large woman wore.

"If you're sure," the younger woman said skeptically.

"I'm sure. I'm not some fine lady who can't do anything for herself." She smiled to take the bite out of her words. Then took the broom, bucket and brush offered and shooed the girls outside. Mae winked at her as she scuttled out the door, obviously please to escape the housework.

Quickly changing into one of her favorite work dresses, made of deep red gingham, Cathleen spent the next hour dusting, sweeping, and scrubbing until the little shack sparkled. It felt good after so long on the road to finally do something useful.

She was tired, but nervous energy seemed to keep her moving. She felt overwhelmed by all of the changes that had occurred so quickly. She was still feeling the shame and hurt of being rejected by her first intended, as well as the sting of being a charity that Benjamin Smith had picked up and carried home.

He was a such a kind man and she determined then and there that she would do her best to take care of him and his home, even while a twinge of guilt at letting the man saddle himself with a woman who couldn't look after herself, made her conscience squirm. She would work hard to ensure she was never a burden.

Cathleen had just finished properly blacking the little stove when the door swung open again and Benjamin stepped in. Smiling he walked to where she stood in the half-light coming from the tiny window and kissed her on the cheek. She had a smudge of blacking by her chin and he wiped it away with his thumb, looking at her fondly.

"I see you've been busy," he said smiling and looking around the one-room hut. "This place hasn't looked this good in a long time." He took in the work she'd done with a sigh. "The girls were a little worried that they'd left you to it though." Benji's dark blue eyes sparkled with pride.

Cathleen's smile was warm and full of appreciation for his words. "It's about time I do something useful," she said.

"I'm sure you'll have plenty of time for that soon enough," the tall man replied. "Now come on up for dinner. Bianca and the girls have whipped up something special," He added offering her his arm.

Quickly washing her hands in the bucket of not so clean water Cathleen dried them on a rag then followed him out the front door, dumping the wash water into a small bush of heather by the door.

***

The noise coming from the two large tables set up on the big back porch was already prodigious as the couple approached. Every member of the Broken J was present and they all seemed to be talking at the same time. Several of them called down introductions to her or just hellos as Benjamin seated her to the left of Joshua who sat at the head of the table and next to lean dark-haired cow puncher she'd seen earlier in the day. She couldn't help but notice how the young man's eyes kept straying across the table the pretty Katie.

A sudden hush fell over the table as the old cattleman bowed his head and said the grace. Cathleen quickly snapped her eyes closed and listened to the prayer while steeling herself for the many questions she knew would come her way.

"How'd you come to meet this old knucklehead?" a thick shouldered man with a crook in his back asked with a smile. He'd been introduced to her as Deeks the blacksmith. She knew he meant no harm with his questions but she could feel the bright color rising along her cheeks.

"Never mind about that," Benjamin said seeing her embarrassment. "I picked her up at the train station just like anyone would with a lovely new mail- order- bride," he added with a wink.

The meal was wonderful but the noise was enough to leave anyone feeling disoriented. Normally reserved in large crowds, Cathleen was managing quite well until suddenly the woman the girls called Nona stepped out from the kitchen carrying an enormous cake, a smile on her face. Nona, still beaming placed the cake in front of Benji and Cathleen with a flourish.

"We all want to make you feel welcome here at the Broken J," she said brightly "I hope you like gingerbread. I just didn't have time to do more."

Cathleen's soft white skin began to flush again as she gazed around at the group of people who had all so warmly welcomed her. The rosy blush deepened creeping up her neck and to the roots of her dark brown hair. It was all too much. She burst into tears, then scrabbled over the bench and raced away.

Benji, his eyebrows almost to his hairline, gazed around him in confusion then shaking his head rose and followed after his wife, while a shocked and confused Nona stared bewilderedly about.

Behind her, Cathleen could hear Bianca Leoné's dazed words and she ran harder.

"Did I say something wrong?" the woman asked quietly. No one laughed at the obvious chagrin on the older woman's face.

"You didn't do anything wrong, Bianca." Joshua offered kindly. "You know how overpowering we can all be at the beginning. You just leave her and Benji to get acquainted and I'm sure everything will be fine."

***

Throwing herself down on the bright quilts of the big bed Cathleen gave in to all of the emotions warring within her. The devastation of rejection, the shame of needing someone to help her, the sorrow that she would never have a man's love. It all crashed over her in waves, mingled with exhaustion.

Behind her, the door creaked open but she did not lift her head. She couldn't bear to see the pity in Benjamin's eyes.

"Cathleen?" His voice was soft, caring. She felt the bed dip as it took his weight and then a large warm hand gently began patting her back and for a moment she felt like laughing hysterically as the bear of a man patted her like one would comfort a child.

They sat there like that for a long time as the shadows grew filling the little house with a gray haze. "You won't be staying here forever you know," the gray-haired man said awkwardly.

Cathleen's pulse quickened as panic threatened to sweep her away. Was he going to take her back to Casper? Had he decided he couldn't bear to be with her even out of pity? She trembled with the thought.

"I have a cabin not far from here and once things are settled around the ranch we'll go there for the winter."

She gasped, suddenly able to breathe again and struggled to sit up.

Benjamin wrapped his arm around the beautiful woman next to him, his heart heavy with sorrow at her distress. Leaning toward him, she laid her head on his shoulder. "I'm sorry if you're not happy," he whispered.

"It's not you Benjamin," she said, her voice soft in the growing darkness. "I just don't want to be a burden to you." She took a deep breath but continued. "I know you only married me out of a sense of pity and it makes me feel like all of this is one big lie." Cathleen hung her head in shame.

"Pity!" Benji replied in shock. "You think I married you out of pity?"

She nodded, her head rubbing slightly against the rough fabric of his shirt, as fresh tears began to spill down her face.

Gently the big man turned her toward him then placing a calloused finger under her chin he lifted her tear-stained face toward him. "I did not marry you out of pity. When I saw you standing there on that train platform all I could think of was that God must have misplaced one of his angels." He smiled at her willing her to understand.

A sad smile crossed Cathleen's face. "Thank you," she said gazing at him, her dark doe-like eyes bright from crying. "You've been so kind. I'm sorry if I embarrassed you tonight."

"You didn't embarrass me at all," he chided. "And don't you worry any about the others either, they know you're plumb wore out from all this traveling. You'll see, soon you'll be just as happy as can be here."

Gently he lowered his head and kissed her. It was a chased kiss, but warm and full of understanding and even though she still knew he didn't want her it made her feel a little better. At least they could be comfortable together if never intimate. It helped.

A gentle knock on the door drew their attention. Cathleen dashed the tears from her face with the back of her hand. "Come in," she called her voice strong even after crying, as she stood from the bed.

Mae popped her head around the door. "Nona said to tell you that the girls are all done with the bath if you'd like to wash," she called into the dark interior of the soddy. "I'll show you if you want to come along."

"Thank you, Mae," Cathleen called from the darkness. "Just give me a minute to get my things together and I'll be right along." Quickly she gathered her nightgown and wrap as well as clean underthings then turned toward the door.

"Wait," Benji called rummaging in the trunk at the foot of the bed before stepping up to her and placing a small package into her hand, kissing her on the head and letting her go.

The small log building that Mae led her to was warm and damp and smelled of soap. Entering Cathleen was shocked to find not one but three large copper tubs spaced across the heavy plank floor.

Next to the outer wall near a small door stood another small potbellied stove like the one in her new little house. Two large buckets of water sat steaming on its top and near the door, a hand pump stuck up through the floor in a bed of stones that let water drain away. Cathleen gasped.

"Everyone says it's pretty special," Mae said with an innocent smile. "I don't know why but that's what they say."

"Thank you, Mae. This is wonderful and thank you for being kind to me." She hugged the spritely girl close for a moment.

The petite girl titled her head making her sheet of black hair fall over her shoulder. "I like you," she stated matter-of-factly, then turned and walked out the door closing it with a snap.

Cathleen quickly stripped her clothes and in only her knickers and camisole carried the buckets of hot water from the stove, pouring their contents into the nearest tub, then filling the bucket from the pump added more until the water was hip-high but still steaming. Carefully, she re-filled the buckets and placed them on the glowing stove.

With a deep sigh, she stripped off the rest of her things and stepped into the warm water. She'd just put one foot in when she remembered the small package that Benjamin had handed her and with a groan she stepped back over to where her clothes hung, pulling it out of her apron pocket. A small rectangular package wrapped in brown-paper appeared in her hand and she carefully unwrapped it to discover a bar of the same soap she'd used at the tiny inn at Casper. A tear pricked at her eyes at the man's thoughtfulness.

This time she climbed into the tub with determination, letting the warm water lap over her hips and legs up to her chest, before sliding down until it nearly reached her chin.

Cathleen stayed that way for a long time. She couldn't remember ever being able to fit so comfortably in a tub. Sitting up again she reached for the bar of sweet-smelling soap and a brush and began to scrub away the days of trail dust and travel.

CHAPTER 6

Feeling refreshed and somewhat more relaxed Cathleen made her way back to the soddy through the warm quiet night. Above bright stars twinkled from a velvet sky. She'd missed the quiet of a country life since leaving the farm. The last couple of weeks in Ohio she'd stayed with Mrs. Schneider the woman who ran the mail-order-bride agency and her house had been in the busy town.

Mrs. Schneider was a kind, if noisy, widow who not only ran the agency but had a small boarding house where single women could stay. She'd been thrilled with preparing Cathleen for her trip West insisting she take the beautiful purple gown as a wedding present. Cathleen smiled thinking of the woman, in her mind, she could still hear Mrs. Schneider's voice.

***

"Oh, you absolutely must take this dress." She'd said her face stern. "It suits you down to a tee with your pale skin and dark hair you'll be stunning. It belonged to my aunt you know, God rest her soul." The widow tapped her chin looking at the purple confection suspended on a hanger. "It's a little out of style now but no one will care. I always thought I'd get around to cutting it down but now I'm glad I didn't. Go on try it on," she fluttered her hands impatiently.

It had been the prettiest thing Cathleen had ever put on and it had fit her perfectly. Still, no matter how long she wore the dress she always felt like a fraud. It was far too fine for a dairymaid and seeing it, everyone assumed she was a fine lady. "Oh, don't you look beautiful." Geneva Schneider had gushed. "I'm sure your groom will be so thrilled he'll whisk you straight to the preacher."

***

"The silly cow," Cathleen muttered, not unkindly, as she reached for the latch on the door of her new home. "She did mean well though." she sighed wistfully.

Leaving the warm confines of the bathhouse Cathleen headed to her new if temporary home. Stepping over the threshold Cathleen was engulfed in the soft glow of an oil lamp burning brightly on the tiny table. Benjamin smiled and rose from a chair near the stove, his bright eyes glowing.

In one step he stood before her gazing down into her dark eyes and before she could register what was happening he was kissing her. Stunned by his kiss she stood there dumbfounded.

He pulled back his hand sliding away from the back of her neck where it had tangled in her still-damp hair. He looked at her a question in his eyes. "If you're too tired…" he began making her eyes grow wide.

Cathleen felt muddled. What was he saying? Was this big kindly man saying he wanted her to share his bed, as a wife? She blinked a moment not sure what to do or say then sighed as he turned away.

"I guess we'd better turn in," Benjamin's whole frame seemed to sag as he turned away from her.

On impulse Cathleen reached out, grabbing his sleeve. "I don't understand," she whispered feeling heat rise up her neck to her cheeks.

The old cowhand turned toward her shock on his face. "What do you mean you don't understand?" His dark blue eyes ran the length of her where she stood in a soft cotton nightgown, a deep maroon warp hanging loosely around her shoulders.

Cathleen felt her whole face glowing with embarrassment, she must match the color of her wrap by now and bright tears pricked her eyes. "I don't understand what you want," she confessed.

Taking her hand in his Benjamin Smith led her to the bed where he sat beside her. His big calloused hand was warm and strong and gave her courage.

"I'm saying..." he swallowed, "I want you to come to bed."

"But why?" she asked, not finding the right words and knowing she was making a mess of things.

Releasing her hand, he scratched his head, did this woman know nothing about what happened between a man and his wife. He opened his mouth to speak but she stopped him with a soft hand on his arm. He turned his head toward her waiting and noticed the bright color rising from just below the neck of her nightgown to her hairline.

"I know what," she said, a shy smile on her lips. "I don't understand why." She fidgeted beside him. "Especially since you only married me out of pity."

If Benji's eyes had bulged any further they would have popped right out of his head. He stared down at the pretty woman next to him where she sat, head hanging, hidden behind a sheet of dark hair traced with white.

Carefully he placed his hand on her cheek and gently pushed the curtain of hair away from her face securing it behind her ear. Then slipping to the floor before her on his knees he placed a large hand on either side of her face forcing her to look at him. Even now with so much on his mind, he noticed how soft her white skin was in contrast to his work brown hands. The sensation warmed him.

"I didn't marry you out of pity," he began. "I took one look at you standing there on that train platform and my heart jumped right out of my chest making me race it up the stairs." He brushed her cheek with his thumb relishing the feel of her silky, milk-white skin.

Even though he had a hand on either side of her face she shook her head in disbelief.

"Cathleen," Benjamin said firmly, "I've been trying my best to give you time to adjust, but I want you in the worst kind of way. You're driving me crazy woman." He smiled to take the heat out of his words but the heat coursing through his veins couldn't be so easily subdued.

She smiled at him sadly and he knew she didn't believe him. Still, he kissed her. His hands swept the hair off of her shoulders, letting its cool strands run through his fingers like a cascade. She didn't resist his kiss, so he deepened it until her hands came up around his neck.

Cathleen liked the feel of her husband's lips on hers. They were warm and surprisingly soft. A small shiver ran down her body as his kisses increased. She was no young miss without knowledge of what went on between a man and a woman but she'd never experienced it before either and she was curious, she suddenly realized she wanted this.

Benjamin's kisses changed and became more demanding as he devoured her mouth brushing her lips with his tongue and sending a new wave of feeling deep to her core. She parted her lips for him and as his tongue stroked the roof of her mouth she wriggled closer only to have him push her back onto the bed before following her there.

***

The next morning, feeling surprisingly rested considering

she'd been awake for long hours the night before, Cathleen rose with a smile on her lips. She was happy that her husband seemed to be pleased with her and that he at least found her attractive enough to desire her physically. She blushed, thinking about what they'd done, she even felt shy returning to the ranch house for breakfast and yet somehow she felt more confident as well.

"Good mornin' darling," Benji said rising and pulling on the clothes he had discarded carelessly the night before and kissing her on the cheek. She blushed prettily and shooed him away while she dressed.

"What will we do today?" she asked, once properly clothed, taking his arm and heading to the house. She felt strange after making a spectacle of herself the night before but hoped that everyone would chalk it up to exhaustion. She felt safe on Benjamin's arm, almost believing that everything would be all right.

"I'll be organizing the crew into groups for hayin' or bringin' cows down into the lower pastures, but I'll stay close ta' home." He offered her a reassuring smile. "I'd rather be with you all day." He waggled his eyebrows making her giggle and blush.

Breakfast was the usual noisy hustle and bustle but at least this morning she felt up to dealing with it. The men discussed the work for the day and the girls were all given jobs and chores to do. She wondered if she should offer to help with the dishes. She still felt conspicuous in the new home.

Feeling more an outsider than ever before in her life, Cathleen lifted her plate from the table and began to stack the dishes. With Benjamin gone off with the other men, she felt out of place and in the way. The women of the Broken J bustled about in a rhythm established over years of practice making her a counterpoint. Each of the lovely girls, even Mae collected dishes scraping the leftovers into a slop bucket then placing them in the big sink, donning aprons, and beginning the routine of the day. She noted that

Katie had gone along with the men while the other girls fell to daily tasks. Cathleen felt at loose ends, what was she supposed to do all day?

"Thank you." Bianca Leoné chirped brightly taking the stack of dishes from Cathleen. "I'm sure you're still tired from your long journey. Why don't you go back to the soddy and have a rest?" She smiled brightly but the words left Cathleen feeling as if she had been dismissed. Once again she was unneeded.

Returning to the little earthen shack she looked around the place trying to think of what she could do. She had cleaned yesterday and since she hadn't cooked in the shack there was nothing to tidy. Her eyes fell on the big wooden trunk where yesterday she'd stored her clothing and personal items. She smiled brightly realizing she would have time to sew.

As the morning wore on a bright sun warmed the outside of the little hut but the inside temperatures remained comfortable. Cathleen sat in the big bed, her bright red skirt furled out around her feet as she utilized the light of the little window to make neat stitches along the bodice of the new dress she had cut out on the table earlier. The bight lilac calico was beautiful and indulged her love for purple.

Dropping her hands into her lap with a sigh she thought of the kind man she had married, who'd insisted on purchasing fabric and other items she'd needed before leaving Casper.

He did seem to be a good man and at least he found her desirable. She blushed feeling her body warm at the thought. She would do her best to be content with that, it was more than she had hoped for. She wasn't a young girl with stars in her eyes anymore. She would count her blessings.

Still, it would be a wonderful thing to be loved. Picking up her sewing again she pushed her dark thoughts away, concentrating on her work.

Later, as the sun passed its zenith, the door to the soddy flew open and Benjamin stepped in a worried expression on his face as he froze just inside the threshold. As the door had swung wide on its hinges banging the wall with a heavy clunk a buzzing rattle permeated the room, raising the small hairs on the back of Cathleen's neck.

The longtime foreman of the Broken J stood perfectly still, his eyes going wide as a large rattlesnake lifted its wedge-shaped head from its coiled body, shaking the rattle on its tail menacingly.

From the corner of his eye, he saw Cathleen climb quietly off the bed her eyes locked on his, and desperately he wanted to scream at her to stay back. His heart raced in his throat as the viper's tongue darted in and out of its mouth trying to pinpoint his location, pulling its head back in preparation to strike.

The sudden whoosh and loud clunk, snap, and clatter of the big iron skillet flying through the air and making a percussive impact with the snake's head had Benjamin Smith throwing his large frame out the door and into the bright sunshine. Quickly jumping to his feet again he dashed back into the soddy pistol at the ready. On the floor near the door, the long form of the rattler writhed and twitched, its broad head shattered by the impact of the skillet.

Benji gaped at his new bride who stood near the stove calmly waiting for the sidewinder to realize it was already dead. She showed no signs of distress or even fear. He blinked at her trying to find words. Finding his voice after several attempts, he opened his mouth. "Are you all right?"

Cathleen offered him a small smile. "Yes, I'm not daft enough to get near the thing though." She began. "My father taught me how to deal with snakes as a child." Her matter of fact words trickled into his brain. "We used to get them around the pastures especially in the spring when calves are very vulnerable to snake bite."

Again Benji blinked at her. "What a woman," he whispered. He was surprised to see the confusion on her face.

"It's just a snake," she offered matter-of-factly. "I've killed dozens of them."

As the writhing form of the snake stopped twitching Benjamin Smith stepped around the table and took his wife in his arms. "You just saved my life," he said then kissed her soundly.

Cathleen clung to him suddenly realizing he truly could have been bitten by the creature, as he let her go she smiled at him mischievously. "I may have saved your life but just look at the mess I've made of my kitchen."

Benji kissed her again.

CHAPTER 7

After being kissed until the blood pounded in her ears Cathleen straightened her dress and looked up into the bright eyes of the man she'd married. "What are you doing here anyway?" she asked. Wondering why he'd come back in the middle of the day.

"You didn't come up for lunch and I thought you might be sick." His eyes were worried.

Cathleen blushed. "I'm afraid I was sewing and lost track of time," she admitted. "I'll go right up to the house and help out now.

"No one was worried about you not helping, they was just worried that something was wrong." He shivered and grasped her hand thinking about the big snake that still lay on the sod floor behind him. If she had started to leave not realizing it was behind the door it could have killed her. Once again he pulled her into his arms. "I'm glad you're all right," he said softly into her ear, making little shivers run from her neck to her toes.

"We'd better get up to the house," Cathleen finally said, "before everyone comes looking for us."

"I'll get this mess cleaned up," the big cowhand offered, giving her hand one more squeeze.

Once Benji had disposed of the snake, lifting it carefully on the head of the shovel and then burying it behind the vegetable garden, he and Cathleen walked to the house hand in hand.

Lunch was winding down as the couple arrived, several people had already left to get back to their chores and Cathleen blushed at their lateness but no one seemed to mind. Instead, they made room at the table and passed the dishes around.

Benji had just filled his plate when he innocently mentioned to Joshua that Cathleen had killed a large rattlesnake in the sod hut, with nothing but a frying pan. Silence fell like a stone as every eye at the table turned toward the couple. Cathleen felt her face go scarlet.

"Don't make a big fuss," she said softly. "It was just a snake."

All at once, everyone was asking questions, the women turned to Cathleen shocked that she hadn't been terrified, while the men bombarded Benji for the details. Once everyone's curiosity had been satisfied Joshua spoke.

"There must be a hole somewhere in the foundation," he stated, obviously thinking the problem through. "With this heat, the critter's probably been coming in there to hunt and now you two moved in he didn't know what to do."

"We've only been using the soddy to store supplies for years," Bianca said still shocked at the discovery. "I'm so sorry you had to go through that dear," she added as if it were her fault.

"Mrs. Leoné…" Cathleen began only to be interrupted by the older woman.

"You call me Bianca like everyone else," she said reaching a hand across the table to pat the other woman.

"Bianca then," Cathleen started again. "I think everyone here has gotten the wrong impression of me." She swallowed looking to Benjamin for support, then continued as he nodded. "I'm just a simple farm girl from Ohio. My father worked on a large dairy farm my whole life and I was no more than a milkmaid. I'm used to keeping house and doing chores just like you, so please don't worry about me." She gazed around the table to be sure that everyone understood. "I've had to kill snakes many times when out watching the cows, so please don't make a fuss."

For a moment everyone was silent then Bianca stood and walking around the table wrapped her arms around Cathleen's shoulders.

"You may think that you are only a simple farm girl but to us, you are the beautiful lady who has made Benji so happy." She paused and smiled. "Not to mention saving his life today. We are so glad to have you here."

A bright tear spilled from Cathleen's eye. "Then I guess you'll let me help with the dishes today," she offered with a grin.

After lunch, the men split up to various tasks while Joshua, Benji, and Isadoro went to the soddy to find and patch the hole the snake had gotten through.

"I'll see you at supper," Benjamin offered, planting a kiss on Cathleen's cheek before leaving.

"You've made him very happy," Bianca spoke sometime later as she dried dishes while Cathleen washed.

"He's a good man," Cathleen replied, "I like him."

"It's always good to like the man you marry," Bianca said with a smile. They both chuckled.

"So how are you finding the Broken J?" The older woman asked and Cathleen found herself opening up for the first time in a long while.

"It's a beautiful place," she began. "I think I could be happy here."

"Did Benji say when you'd be going to his cabin?"

"No, he only mentioned it. Is it far?" Suddenly she was afraid of being completely alone with the man who was a virtual stranger. What would it be like to only have Benji to talk to all day? What if he didn't like the woman she was? She shivered at the thought.

"It's not far at all, just over the creek and up the hill in a grove of trees. I'm sure you'll get over here all the time. Either way, me and the girls will drop in now and then." She smiled as if she liked the idea.

"I am sorry about not being here to help prepare lunch," Cathleen offered out of the blue.

"Well I think enough happened that it's understandable," Bianca chided.

"Oh no, it wasn't the snake that made me late. I was sewing and completely lost track of time."

The older woman took the last plate from Cathleen, dipped it in the clean water of the second washtub then wiped it with a cloth before speaking again.

"You like to sew?"

"I love it," Cathleen replied with a big grin. "My mother taught me before she passed away. I'm afraid I haven't had much time recently though." She glanced down at her rather worn attire.

"We'll make some new curtains for the soddy together then," Bianca said already excited about the thought. "It always seems that there is just so much to keep up with here at the ranch some things get neglected."

After the dishes were washed and the kitchen tidied Bianca encouraged Cathleen to return to her own home to continue work on her dress. "I've got more than enough help around the kitchen," She offered kindly then with a wink shouted for the girls to come and help her.

As the days wore on at the Broken J Cathleen began to feel more confident. She could tell that Benjamin liked her and being alone with him was no longer so awkward. He was attentive and seemed to enjoy spending time with her. After the episode with the snake and her pronouncement that she wanted to do her fair share she even felt more a part of the ranch and was quickly becoming friends with Bianca Leoné'. It was a joy to have another woman to talk to. She also reveled in the time she had to sew and found time to do it every day.

Cathleen had been sitting on the bed sewing again when a soft tap sounded at the door. Glancing out the window to check the time she determined that it couldn't be supper-time yet then scooted off of the bed, wondering if Mae was popping in again before opening the door.

Katie stood at the door in a lovely yellow dress, her golden hair piled on her head in a loose bun.

"I just made fresh cookies and thought you might like some," Katie said in greeting, holding out a small plate covered by a cloth.

"That'd be lovely," The other woman said and directed Katie to the small two-person table by the minuscule cook stove. "Won't you come in for tea."

"I hope you're settling in all right now." Katie's words were polite as she placed the cookies on the table and sat in a chair.

Cathleen's soft laugh was her initial reply, as she placed cups and saucers on the table then pulled a tin of tea off of a shelf. "I won't say it's been easy but yes I think I am. It's such a beautiful place and Benjamin says we'll be moving to his cabin as soon as the snow arrives."

"Oh, I hadn't thought of that," Katie said as she watched Cathleen sit and pour the tea. "Isn't it hard being so far away from everyone, family, and friends, I mean?"

"I don't have any family left," Cathleen said wistfully "and as for friends, I think I'll make my fair share here. life is all about your attitude and not your circumstances."

Katie pondered the other woman's words while she munched a sugar cookie. She found that she truly liked Cathleen and that despite the woman's bumpy start as a member of the Broken J's odd family, she thought that someday they could be real friends. Cathleen was quiet and reserved, but also had a quick humor hidden just below the surface.

"I don't think I could ever just leave home like you did," Katie began, thinking out loud as she sipped her tea. "I mean my whole family is here and they need me. I have Pa, and all of my sisters, and Nona, Grans, and Ye-ye Chen Lou aren't getting any younger. They need me to look after things."

"I'm proud to see a young woman with a sense of responsibility," Cathleen said, smoothing her skirts and looking across the table at her young guest.

"But what does it mean to care for your family? Before my father passed…" she paused taking a steadying breath "… he insisted that the only thing that would make him rest easy was to know I was taken care of. It's the biggest reason I decided to become a mail-order-bride."

For a moment her eyes took on a faraway look. "Sometimes, what we think of as being selfish or self-serving is really what our family wants for us. What they want is for us to be happy and safe, that's all."

For some reason Cathleen's words made Katie feel uncomfortable. She had always known her place. Her whole life she'd known that as the oldest she had to watch over her family and see that they had everything they needed. Her wants and desires were secondary to theirs. Up until recently, everything she had ever wanted had been right here; she'd been content, happy, satisfied in her role. Why did she feel so restless now? Finishing her tea, she thanked her new aunt for the visit and excused herself. But once she left the cheery confines of the tiny sod shack she couldn't shake her feeling of unease.

***

Cathleen pondered her visit with Katie. The girl needed to follow her heart, but even as she thought of it she wondered if she could follow her own. Every day she was becoming more aware of her feelings for Benjamin Smith. Initially, she had thought he was simply a kind man who wouldn't leave a woman stranded and alone, but now she wasn't sure. Did she dare hope he could care for her?

As the days turned into weeks an easy routine was established and Cathleen felt useful as she helped out in the kitchen or with the mending. Each night after supper the family would retire to the parlor to read or do mending and other small jobs. Then she and Benjamin would escape to the soddy where she'd make tea and they would spend time sitting together before turning in.

Tonight was no different but instead of easy conversation, Benjamin seemed distracted.

"Benjamin is everything all right?" she asked after several minutes of silence.

He raised his eyes to hers. "I'm just thinking about Katie and Will," he replied.

"They do seem to be smitten with each other don't they." Cathleen smiled. "I don't know why they resist so hard."

"None of us knows what to do for them," Benji continued. "You'd think two young people would just sort of grow together. When Josh came up with this idea of findin' husbands for his girls..." he stopped suddenly realizing what he'd said and smiled at the surprise on Cathleen's face.

"He didn't?" she gaped, a bright smile spreading across her face.

Benji nodded. "We didn't know what else to do. The girls are here and not only don't we want them to go away, some like Katie, couldn't be pried off the place. We had to do something."

Taking her hand, he explained the situation as best he could, delighting in her giggles over the whole affair.

Suddenly Cathleen stopped laughing, and Benji looked up into her serious face.

"What about us Benjamin?" she asked, her eyes steady.

"What do you mean?" he questioned, bewildered.

"Are we growing together?" Cathleen's heart raced even as she boldly asked the words.

"I don't know how we'll get along in your cabin all alone if we're not," she added, hope warring with doubt in her breast.

Benji's eyes softened as he gazed at her. Could she not know how much he cared for her? Hadn't he shown her again and again?

"Are you saying you don't care for me Cathleen?" he asked softly afraid of the answer while desperate to know.

"I do care for you." The woman across from him spoke, her voice just a whisper, her dark eyes glowing now. "That's what I'm so afraid of."

Taking her hand, he pulled her upright and brought her around the table until she rested in his arms. The feel of her had become so familiar to him. Her soft curves, her silky hair, the smell of honey and lemon on her skin. He loved her plump folds and each time he took her in his arms he felt like a young man again.

"Don't you know how much I care for you?" he asked resting his chin on her head as she leaned into him, he felt more than heard her response.

Holding her close he drew her toward the bed, pulling her down onto the mattress beside him. "Do you believe in love at first sight?" he finally asked.

"I think it's something you just read about in stories," Cathleen answered, her voice shaky.

"That's what I thought as well," his voice was rough. "Until that day in Casper when I saw you standing by the depot."

Cathleen gasped, could he be saying what she thought? What did he mean?

"The moment my eyes lit on you I was smitten." Benji continued. "I couldn't think of anything else and almost got run down by a mule team crossing the street just to get to you. There's no other way to explain it. As soon as I saw you my heart was gone."

Cathleen pulled away from him. "Are you saying you love me Benjamin Smith?" her voice was startled, hopeful.

"Yes, but apparently I'm not doing a very good job of it." He chortled before looking her in the eye.

"Cathleen Malone Smith, I love you and I'm just praying to the good Lord that He will let you come to feel something for me along the way."

Cathleen giggled even as tears began to stream from her eyes. "Oh Ben, I love you too. I thought you were just being kind to me, that you were the sort of man who wouldn't leave a woman stranded and alone. I've been falling in love with you this whole time and was so worried you'd get fed up with me."

Benji wiped her tears away with a callused thumb. "I'll never get tired of you," he said leaning in to kiss her. "I love everything about you and if you don't believe that let me prove it." He chuckled again then fell to kissing her.

Hours later, Cathleen gazed at the oil lamp still burning brightly on the small table in her new home. She knew she should get up and put it out but she didn't want to move from where she lay wrapped in her husband's arms feeling warm, content, and loved.

EPILOGUE

Cathleen walked into her new home. The cabin was beautiful in her eyes. Simple but well set up. It wasn't as grand as the big ranch house at the Broken J and even if it didn't have an indoor pump, it was hers.

She smiled at Ben. Somehow she'd lost the need to be formal with him, shortening his proper name. There were other names she called him now as well, and she blushed thinking about the endearments.

"What do you think?" The man himself spoke concern evident in his voice.

"It's perfect," she replied confidently. "It does need a good scrub though," she added, but not critically.

"I built it ages ago thinking that someday I'd move here but it never seemed like the right time, there always seemed to be a little bit more to do on the ranch. Now with Will settled as the new foreman and things changing on the ranch I feel like I can call it home." He smiled stepping close, hoping she'd be happy.

Cathleen turned and wrapped her arms around him. "I truly love it, Ben. I know we'll be happy here."

To Benji's surprise, she turned and pulled a picture frame out of her valise then scanned the room. "I know just where to put this," she said walking toward the fireplace on the far wall of the three-room log cabin and propping the frame on the mantle.

Benji squinted to look at it and was surprised to see that it was the letter from the man who'd left her standing all alone at the train depot in Casper a few months ago.

"What in thunder are you putting that up for?" he blustered suddenly feeling annoyed.

"It's a reminder," Cathleen said turning and laying a hand along his cheek. "It reminds me every day that God's plans are perfect even when we don't understand. If I hadn't answered that add for a mail-order-bride and if that man hadn't rejected me, I never would have met the love of my life."

She leaned toward him kissing him softly.

"I guess I understand." Benji whispered pulling her closer, "I'm lucky that man was so foolish."

The End

More from this author
Sign up for my Newsletter and get a free book! Subscribe **or follow on** Bookbub at Facebook & AllAuthor

Other Books by this Author:

From the Cattleman's Daughters

Katie   Isabella

Fiona   Alexis

Meg   Mae

Cattleman's Daughters Companions

DANNI ROAN

Cathleen

The Redemption of Rachel

Sean's Secret Heart

Mel

Sweet Annie

Joan

Tales from Biders Clump

Christmas Kringle

Quil's Careful Cowboy

Bruno's Belligerent Beauty

Tywyn's Troubles

A Teaching Touch

Prissy's Predicament

Lucinda's Luck

Ferd's Fair Favor

The Travels of Titus

Winter's Worth

Strong Hearts: Open Spirits

Maggie's Valley   Sadina's Stocking

Celestre's Song   Beloved Beulah

Whispers in Wyoming

Love Letters & Home

Counting Kadence

Mercy's Light

Falling Forward

Racing Destiny

Baby be Mine

The Ornamental Match Maker

Carousel Horse Christmas

Loose Goose Christmas

Pineapple Persuasion

July's Jubilant Christmas Jumble

Shutter Shock Christmas in July

Brides of Needful Texas

Daliah

Prim

Peri

Beth

Ruth

If you enjoyed this book check out more books by Danni Roan at Amazon Or follow me on Facebook, Twitter, Bookbub & AllAuthor

If you'd like to get updates on my work, see special sneak peeks and be entered in special contests sign up for my newsletter on my webpage or my amazon author page

For more amazing Western Historical Romance join me and my friends at Pioneer Hearts a Facebook group for readers like you.

DEAR READER,

Thank you for choosing to read my book. I hope you have enjoyed it as much as I've enjoyed writing it. If you enjoyed the story please feel free to leave a review wherever you purchased the book. Leaving a review will help me and prospective readers to know what you liked about this book. It is an opportunity for your voice to be heard and for you to tell others why the story is worth a read.

ABOUT THE AUTHOR

Danni Roan, a native of western Pennsylvania, spent her childhood roaming the lush green mountains on horseback. She has always loved westerns and specifically western romance and is thrilled to be part of this exciting genre. She has lived and worked overseas with her husband and tries to incorporate the unique quality of the people she has met throughout the years into her books.

Danni currently lives in her thirty-six foot RV with her husband and is traveling the United States to see this beautiful country and experience its history first hand.

Danni and her 'every-day-hero' have one son who is attending college and finding his way as his crazy parents experience the author's life along with life on the road.

As a Christian Danni, believes strongly that God brings new challenges, and blessings into one's life to help them grow and she hopes that her words were both an encouragement and inspiration to you.

Made in the USA
Las Vegas, NV
21 August 2021